BOBBY IS DEAD

by MARTY MATFESS

BOBBY IS DEAD

SPECIAL NOTE

SPECIAL NOTE ON SONGS AND RECORDINGS

Cover Art and Book Design: Jonathan Cook
First Edition: March 2024
ISBN: 978-1-964045-00-9

A tale of love, lust, and getting shot in the head.

BOBBY IS DEAD by Marty Matfess premiered at Le Chat Noir Theatre, located at 304 8th Street, Augusta, GA in September 2019. It was directed by Krys Bailey. The cast was as follows:

ANNIE .... Dani Westman
BOBBY .... Jaye Starkes
CHRIS .... Michael Silvio Fortino
DANIEL .... Ben Evans
ELIZABETH .... Andrea Collins

BOBBY IS DEAD

CHARACTERS

ANNIE
Female; vapid; self-centered but not altogether unlikeable.

BOBBY
Male; ex-boyfriend of Annie; unemployed; lives in his mother's basement; constantly feels sorry for himself; tries to be tough but his ego is easily bruised.

CHRIS
Male; in love with Annie; our everyman.

DANIEL
Male; police officer; clean-cut; likely more conventionally attractive than Chris.

ELIZABETH
Female; Daniel's sister; kind of a badly dressed 'manic pixie dream girl' trope, where she is also sarcastic, a bit aggressive and (purposefully) weird.

PLACE
Annie's house.

TIME
Now.

AUTHOR NOTES

Time is now, place is here. No accents are required, and add whatever regionalism is required for the show. Numbers and ages which can be changed without any permission to fit casting. Exception: Elizabeth MUST be over 20. She is (and has been) an adult and has full agency over her body and her choices.

I use "Fuck" a lot in the dialog. (34 times at last count) Directors can switch this to bone, screw, do, boink or whatever other words you want. Probably not suitable for a high school show.

This was originally written for a black box theater, so set design is minimal. For sure you will need a living room area, an 'exit' that leads to the hallway and interior rooms. A front door 'entrance' for people to come into the apartment, and (most important) a living room closet big enough to fit a dead guy in (and a way to get him off stage once he is dead … otherwise he'll be in there for a long time.)

ACT ONE
Scene 1

Annie's living room.

At rise, Annie enters from the hallway with a cell phone in her hand. She does a voice-to-text with her phone. As she records and sends her texts in this scene, she changes out of her dress, leaving it on the floor. She then tries on a t-shirt, changes her mind, throws it on the floor and then puts on another t-shirt and jeans. She can also apply makeup and primp a bit in a mirror while doing this.

On another lit part of the stage, we see Bobby playing video games in his mom's basement. He's getting the texts but ignoring them.

ANNIE. *(To her phone.)* Hey Bobby, I've been thinking a lot about us lately. I'm sure you've noticed I've not been fully present in our relationship lately-period. The thing is, I don't really see where 'we' are going in this whole boyfriend/girlfriend thing. *(Thinks.)* Remember when we kind of discussed seeing other people, and I kind of wanted to, and you kind of didn't. Well, I kind of did go ahead and see other people-period-I mean, it's not like I really cheated on you … because we totally discussed seeing other people-comma, even though you didn't want to. … I did so that makes it ok. … I discussed it with Chris and he thinks the best thing I can do for both of our sakes is to break up with you-period. He says that it's the only way to be fair to you-period. I know you hate Chris, and I know you're totally jealous of our friendship, but he supports my decision-Period. He thinks we should see other people. *(She sends the text. After a moment, she looks back at her phone to reread what she sent. She starts another voice to text after reading.)* I'm not sure if I was totally clear in that last text-Period. I think we should see other people and stop seeing each other. *(She sends the text. Then grabs a box marked "Bobby" from the closet and starts putting his belongings in it. Maybe even debating about an item or two, if he should get it back or not. As she loads things into the box, she starts another voice to text.)* I think that might have been harsher than I wanted it to be. I do still love you- period. I want this break up to be as easy as possible. ... I put your stuff in a box and left it in the front closet-period. Hey, would you mind leaving your key on the coffee table when you come pick it up-question mark? ... Could you come early this afternoon, because I have some plans tonight and well, it would be best if this were over quickly. *(She sends the text. And then immediately starts another.)* Also, would you mind deleting those naked selfies? That would be good too. *(She sends the text. After a moment, she starts another text.)* I really do love you Bobby, I just, I just want so much more than you'll ever be able to offer me-period. Cause you're kind of unemployed-Period. And you don't have much direction in life-period. And you're not a very good dresser-period. And kind of clumsy in bed. And you still live with your parents. And Chris says I deserve better. So lets just be friends. *(She sends the text. Then she places the "Bobby" box in the closet and exits. Bobby, finally breaking from his game; looks at the texts. Eyes go wide as he reads.)*

BOBBY. *(As he exits.)* MOM! I need the car keys!

    Blackout.

ACT ONE
Scene 2

Annie's living room.
At rise, Chris enters from a half opened front door.

CHRIS. Knock knock. Anyone home? Annie? Annie, you home? *(Enters the room, searches the place.)* Annie? *(Picks up dress off the floor.)* Annie, you're such a slob. *(Neatly lays it on the arm of the couch. Then picks up a t-shirt off the floor.)* Lord, what are we going to do with you? Would you even know what a hamper is for? *(Brings the shirt to a hamper, begins to place it in, sees a pair of cotton panties. He picks them up; stares longingly at them. He sniffs them when he hears a noise at the door.)*

BOBBY. *(Outside door.)* Annie? Annie? Are you in there? *(Enters as Chris jams the panties back in the hamper).* Oh, what the fuck, man …?

CHRIS. What? Me? What? I wasn't doing anything. What are …

BOBBY. Why the fuck are you here? Why the fuck are you always here?

CHRIS. I'm Annie's best friend. That's why I'm here.

BOBBY. Sure you are. I know I've not pushed this before, but today is different. Let's get something straight, dude, you're not here because she's your friend. You're in love with her.

CHRIS. I am not. We are FRIENDS.

BOBBY. She's a friend you want to fuck.

CHRIS. We're friends. Nothing more.

BOBBY. Dude, admit it, you're happy she broke up with me.

CHRIS. Wait, what? She broke up with you?

BOBBY. Don't act like you didn't know. You knew.

CHRIS. No, for real, I didn't know. I mean, we discussed it, but … she broke up with you? When?

BOBBY. An hour ago. By text.

CHRIS. Text?

BOBBY. Text.

CHRIS. Wow. That's harsh.

BOBBY. Like you didn't fucking know. You knew. Hell, she even said you knew. She said you told her she should see other people.

CHRIS. Well, I … she said she was unhappy, so I told her what any friend would tell another friend that's unhappy.

BOBBY. Any friend that wants to fuck that friend.

CHRIS. Not true.

BOBBY. Whatever man. She said you knew all about her dating other guys.

CHRIS. Wait … what?

BOBBY. She's been cheating on me. She said you knew. I thought we were friends.

CHRIS. Friends? You fucking hate me. *(Beat.)* She's been dating other people?

BOBBY. You didn't know? For real?

CHRIS. No.

BOBBY. Guess she's been cheating on both of us then.

CHRIS. She wasn't cheating on me.

BOBBY. Dude, admit it. You in love with her.

CHRIS. I -

BOBBY. You love her.

CHRIS. I -

BOBBY. You want to fuck her.

CHRIS. Look I -

BOBBY. You want to kiss her.

CHRIS. No, I -

BOBBY. You want to kiss her deeply

CHRIS. Hey, no I -

BOBBY. You want to nuzzle her boobies.

CHRIS. *(Less convincing each time.)* No. I -

BOBBY. You want to go muff diving in her treasure chest.

CHRIS. No.

BOBBY. You want to suck her toes.

CHRIS. Wait … what? No. Eww, gross.

BOBBY. But the rest is true

CHRIS. I don't -

BOBBY. Just admit it.

CHRIS. No I …

BOBBY. Dude … with me out of the picture, you can finally have her.

CHRIS. *(Stuttering.)* I just … she just … she …?

BOBBY. *(Reassuring.)* It's ok. It's over with us. She dumped me. So, It's ok. Just, admit it. You've kept hanging around because you want her. Maybe you won't say you want to fuck her, but you're in love, and you've probably been in love with her for a long time. So let's get it off your chest man. Say it. You'll feel better. You're in love with her.

CHRIS. *(Considers.)* I am.

BOBBY. *(Statement.)* And you're happy she dumped me.

CHRIS. No, I …

BOBBY. Admit it.

CHRIS. Ok. Yes, I'm happy she dumped you. *(Bobby pulls out a gun; points it right at Chris's head.)*

BOBBY. I fucking knew it. All along you're all like Mr. Nice Guy, but the whole time you're just hanging out on the sidelines waiting for a chance at her.

CHRIS. What the fuck, dude? Why do you have a gun? What the actual FUCK?! Put it away.

BOBBY. *(Mocking.)* Dude, why do you have a gun? *(Normal.)* Why do you think? Because it's not right that she dumped me by text. WHO FUCKING DOES THAT? Seriously … who? You know who? That ungrateful twat that took my love and then sent me away. What did I do to deserve this? *(No response.)* Well?

CHRIS. You want an answer?

BOBBY. YES I WANT AN ANSWER!

CHRIS. And you think I'm going to give you an answer with a gun pointed at me?

BOBBY. HOW ABOUT YOU GIVE ME AN ANSWER OR I START FUCKING SHOOTING?

CHRIS. Ok, she's a horrible, selfish, vain, little whore?

BOBBY. *(Lowering gun.)* Go on …

CHRIS. She only cares about herself. And things and clothes and money.

BOBBY. Exactly.

CHRIS. And you deserve someone better. *(Bobby sits down; places the gun on the table next to him.)*

BOBBY. I'm never going to find anyone better.

CHRIS. *(Trying to be sincere.)* Hey man, you will. You'll get over this. I promise. And then you'll see the world for what it can be, a beautiful place. *(Standing behind bobby, so he can't see this is total bullshit.)* And you'll find happiness. You'll find a sweet girl who can appreciate you for who you are.

BOBBY. No. That's not how this plays out.

CHRIS. How does this play out?

BOBBY. I'm just gonna get my stuff and put it in my car.

CHRIS. Good.

BOBBY. And then, I'm going to come back inside and wait for her.

CHRIS. What for?

BOBBY. For answers. For apologies. For closure.

CHRIS. Ok. You deserve that. But maybe without the gun?

BOBBY. Then I'm going to tell her how you're in love with her. I'm going to make sure she knows exactly the type of person you are.

CHRIS. *(Indignant.)* The type of person who is a friend?

BOBBY. The type of person who digs through her dirty laundry to sniff her panties. *(Off his look.)* What, you think I didn't see you?

CHRIS. She won't believe you.

BOBBY. She will. You know why? Because deep down she already knows it.

CHRIS. The fuck are you talking about.

BOBBY. You think she's stupid? You think she doesn't see the way you look at her? You think she buys the whole 'best friend' ruse? Deep down, she's always known. Girls always know. She's just using you. I just have to tip the scales a tiny bit and she'll see the truth for what it is.

CHRIS. No way.

BOBBY. No? I bet in your fantasy she eventually figures out that you've been the right man all along, and it all ends with a warm kiss and a loving embrace. Except the reality is, she's already replaced me, and not with you buddy, and if you ever sat her down and told her you're in love with her she'd act like you've betrayed her, and she'll never forgive you.

CHRIS. You don't know that.

BOBBY. Yes, yes I do. So do you. Tic toc buddy. Times up for you.

CHRIS. You're not going to ruin everything! She won't … she won't buy it.

BOBBY. She will. You know something funny? In those old movies where the jilted boyfriend says "If I can't have her, no one can" … that's how I was feeling when I came over. But now that I think about it, my feeling is "If I can't have her, neither can Chris."

CHRIS. Dude … why?

BOBBY. Because. Because you've always been in her ear. "Quit loaning him money, he'll never pay you back."

CHRIS. You never did.

BOBBY. "He's unemployed, he lives with his parents, he works part time at Dairy Queen."

CHRIS. Oh, boo fucking hooo. All of that is true.

BOBBY. Maybe, but, like I said … if I can't have her, neither can you.

CHRIS. Just … don't.

BOBBY. Sorry man. Your little game ends tonight.

CHRIS. Don't do this. You're going to ruin everything.

BOBBY. Payback. Now maybe you can stop being a little bitch and man up. Get a woman of your own. Stop trying to scam someone else's girl. *(He goes to the closet, opens the door.)* If I can't have her, you can't have her. Time to move on Chris, and stop being such a little pussy boy. Time to man up. *(Bends down to get the "Bobby" box.)*

CHRIS. How's this for manning up? *(He gets the gun from the table; holds it awkwardly while pointing it at Bobby. It goes off, and Bobby falls. Chris screams like a high-pitched musical theater fan, surprised and shocked it went off. A long-stunned silence.)* Oh shit. … oh shit … oh shit oh shit. *(Puts gun on table.)* Bobby? You ok there buddy? *(Looks.)* Definitely not ok. *(Begins to pace.)* Not your best moment there Chris … not your best moment at all. What to do what to do what to do … goddammit Chris, you've seen enough true crime stories to think this through … what's step 1? Of course … hide the body. *(He shoves the rest of Bobby's body/legs into the closet and shuts the door.)* Ok. Not a great hiding spot, but it'll do for now. Step 2. Wipe the gun clean of prints. *(Picks up gun; looks around the room for a rag; blindly grabs something out of clothes hamper and begins to wipe gun clean of prints. Realizes he's using the panties from before. Holds them up.)* You're the whole reason I'm in this mess in the first place. *(Sniffs them, then sniffs the gun. Puts the panties down in the hamper.)* Seriously Chris, you have issues. And now I've touched the gun again. *(Grabs the panties again; wipes the gun down again, then wraps the gun in the panties and puts it in the drawer. Begins pacing.)* This is bad … really bad. I mean … oh hey Annie, how was your day? Oh mine? Mine was good. I mean, I shot bobby, yep, he's just dead in your closet. Why yes Annie, I do know how much that means to you! Make out? Now … well, I mean, if you insist, I suppose a small bit of cuddling and canoodling would be perfectly fine. Seeing as I am going to spend a lot of time in jail for this, perhaps we should go to the next logical step? Why yes, I would be honored to make love to you Annie! *(Beat.)* Oh my god Chris … What the ever loving FUCK is wrong with you????? More like *(Impersonating Annie.)* "Oh my god, you killed Bobby, now he'll never pay me back the money he owes me. I am going to hate you forever". Think Chris, think … what are you going to do? *(Annie comes in through the front door, seems unsurprised to see Chris there.)*

ANNIE. Who are you talking to?

CHRIS. What? Huh? Oh, Annie! Sorry, just, talking to myself.

ANNIE. Are you ok? You seem a little, umm pale?

CHRIS. I'm ok, it's been kind of a

ANNIE. *(Interrupting.)* You wouldn't believe the day I've had. Simply dreadful.

CHRIS. Oh no, are you ok? *(Goes in for a hug, realizes she's about to hang her coat in the closet, backs off).*

ANNIE. *(Clueless about the dead body.)* I finally did it. I packed all of Bobby's things and broke up with him.

CHRIS. My god, that must have been difficult for you. *(Pulls her away from the closet).*

ANNIE. *(Overly dramatic.)* It wasn't easy, but I came to the realization that I was simply better off without him.

CHRIS. I've been saying that for months.

ANNIE. I know, but I just wasn't … ready, you know?

CHRIS. Did he take it ok?

ANNIE. I'm sure it killed him. I mean, I tried to be a sensitive as I could in the breakup note I sent, but it's so hard to convey emotion in text … you know? Like "it's over, winky face".

CHRIS. For real? You broke up with him in a text?

ANNIE. Well doing it by snapchat would be rude, I mean,

what if he wanted to re-read it to understand? And doing it in person would be out of the question. You know how anxious I get about things like that.

CHRIS. Yes, you are a fragile flower.

ANNIE. You really get me.

CHRIS. I do. I don't think there is a person alive who gets you better than I get you. *(Annie is looking at her phone, ignoring him.)* I want to get you even more. I really love the idea of getting you.

ANNIE. *(Looking at phone, so the line goes past her).* He never replied. I wonder if he came to get his things. Let me see if he got his stuff out of the closet.

CHRIS. *(Vaulting over the couch.)* No, I'll check. You've had a rough day! *(Runs to the door, opens and closes the closet quickly.)* Nope. It's all still there.

ANNIE. Damn.

CHRIS. I'm sure he'll get it eventually.

ANNIE. Chris, we need to talk. About us.

CHRIS. I couldn't agree more Annie.

ANNIE. I've been keeping something from you Chris. Feelings I've been having.

CHRIS. Me too Annie. I've been keeping things from you.

ANNIE. A short time ago, when I was questioning my feelings for Bobby, you encouraged me to think PAST my relationship with him, and to look around and see if there was something better for me on the horizon.

CHRIS. YES! I remember.

ANNIE. And you even said that if I just looked around, I'd find someone that would be better for me.

CHRIS. Yes. *(Taking her hand.)* Yes exactly.

ANNIE. You said "just look around, there is probably the right guy, right in front of your face."

CHRIS. Yes, Annie, yes.

ANNIE. And that's exactly what I did. Once I opened my eyes it became so clear to me.

CHRIS. Clear.

ANNIE. Few weeks ago, I was getting my morning caramel mocha cappuccino and there was a police officer behind me in line, and he was simply stunning.

CHRIS. Uh huh.

ANNIE. And so I bought him a coffee, and well we … we've started seeing each other.

CHRIS. *(Taking back his hands.)* Uh huh.

ANNIE. I know, I know you're angry. After all, we are best friends! And I kept it a secret from you. Best friends deserve better than that. It's just, I felt so guilty about cheating on Bobby.

CHRIS. *(Beat.)* Don't be so hard on yourself. Cheating is such a strong word, I mean, you've only gone on a few dates, right? It's not like you've had sex with the guy.

ANNIE. Oh no. We've had sex. Lots! The really good kind too. You know. Kind of dirty, kind of forbidden.

CHRIS. Oh.

ANNIE. I mean, the guy has his own set of handcuffs. What girl can resist that?

CHRIS. Certainly not you.

ANNIE. Exactly! Oh Chris, I knew you'd understand. *(Bringing his hand to her chest.)* I'm so glad to get this off my chest. I swear I couldn't keep it a secret another minute, my head was about to explode.

CHRIS. There's a lot of that going around lately.

ANNIE. And I'm so glad you're here RIGHT NOW. *(Pause.)* Why are you here by the way?

CHRIS. I came to return your "Love actually" DVD.

ANNIE. Oh god, I love that movie.

CHRIS. *(Bland.)* Ya, I really like the part when the guy confesses he's in love with his best friends wife.

ANNIE. Huh … oh but I was saying. He's coming over here now.

CHRIS. The Policeman?

ANNIE. Yes, my own personal law enforcement officer!

CHRIS. Does he know about … Bobby?

ANNIE. Yes, silly. He's the one that made me break it off with him. He felt like what we were doing was wrong.

CHRIS. How did YOU feel?

ANNIE. M'eh …

CHRIS. So he's the reason you broke up with Bobby.

ANNIE. Uh huh.

CHRIS. No other reason?

ANNIE. I mean, Bobby and I agreed to see other people. Well, at least half of us did. But Daniel wanted a committed relationship. We're dating.

CHRIS. You and Officer Daniel?

ANNIE. Technically he is a Lieutenant.

CHRIS. Lieutenant Daniel?

ANNIE. Yes.

CHRIS. *(Deadpan.)* Lieutenant Dan?

ANNIE. He should make captain soon. And the best part is, *(Looking at watch.)* if you stick around for a few minutes, you'll get to meet him. It's an important night. His sister is in town, on a break *(She does air quotes.)* from school.

CHRIS. *(Air quotes.)* From school?

ANNIE. Dan always does it like that. Maybe it's a vocational school? Anyway, he wants us to meet, and then we're going to dinner. I really wanna to make a great impression. Will you help me pick an outfit?

CHRIS. Of course. *(Annie exits down the hallway. Chris speaks to himself.)* Are you fucking kidding me? Seriously … are you fucking kidding me. Let's just get everything in perspective. You love Annie. She was screwing Bobby. You killed bobby. Bobby is dead. Over there. In the closet. And now Annie is screwing a cop. Who is on his way here. Chris, if I were going to council you on this, I might tell you that being infatuated with Annie is not the healthiest thing you can do with your life. Just saying, maybe now is the time to move on. *(Annie emerges from the closet wearing red matching bra and panties. And has in each hand a dress on a hanger.)*

ANNIE. Thank god you're here to help me with this. Tonight is important. Which one. *(She is holding each outfit off to one side.)* Black … *(Moves the black in front of her.)* or Red *(Moves the red in front of her.)*

CHRIS. Huh.

ANNIE. *(Same motions.)* What do you think? Black or red?

CHRIS. Ummm … I think red. Wait … hold them apart again … *(She does.)* Yes. Red. Red for sure. *(Annie is pleased but stops to look at a mirror on the way out, putting both dresses in front of her. Chris stares at her backside nonstop until she exits.)* So … not sure moving on is going to happen anytime soon. Memo to self: pick up some lotion on the way home. *(Thinks.)* Another memo to self. Probably should do something about the dead guy in the closet. *(A doorbell rings/or knock at the door)*

ANNIE. *(From offstage.)* Oh my god, that's Dan! Will you get that … unless it's bobby. If it's bobby, hand him the box in the closet and then get him to leave. If it's Dan, invite him and his sister in. I'll just be a minute. *(Chris opens the door to admit Dan, who is dressed impeccably; creased pants, pressed shirt, hair neat, perhaps in a suit.)*

CHRIS. Come on in. You must be Lieutenant Daniel. *(In a voice.)* Lieutenant Dan, you got legs.

DANIEL. *(Putting hand to where a gun would be if he were in uniform.)* Bobby?

CHRIS. Chris.

DANIEL. Oh. Chris. Her Gay Best Friend.

CHRIS. I'm … not gay.

DANIEL. Really?

CHRIS. Ya … really.

DANIEL. Wow, I'm sorry. It's just the way Annie described you, I just assumed.

CHRIS. Wait … did Annie say I'm gay? Does Annie think I'm …

DANIEL. *(Interrupting.)* Oh, no, no no … not at all. Well, maybe. No. She never said you weren't gay, she just described you as sensitive, always there for her. So I assumed that …

CHRIS. I'm not gay.

DANIEL. I believe you, but you do watch *Say Yes to the Dress* and *Real Housewives*.

CHRIS. *(Looks over to the drawer where the gun was placed.)* That doesn't make me gay!

DANIEL. I suppose not.

CHRIS. Straight guys can like bitchy women and wedding dresses.

DANIEL. Really? I mean … I guess so.

CHRIS. So … straight.

DANIEL. Got it. *(Looks over to see Annie emerge from the hallway in a little black dress.)* Oh, there you are.

Wow, you look amazing. That dress is …

ANNIE. *(Twirling.)* This old thing? You like it? Chris helped pick it out.

CHRIS. *(Salty.)* It was between that one and the red one. I liked the red one.

ANNIE. Chrissy-poo, I didn't have good shoes to go with the red one. But the Black one got the reaction I was hoping for! *(Chris is again looking where the gun was placed.)*

DANIEL. You look amazing.

ANNIE. You look great too!

DANIEL. Oh, let me get Elizabeth. Guys, She's on a little break *(Air quotes.)* from school.

CHRIS. *(Air quotes.)* From school?

DANIEL. *(Ignoring him.)* And she's a little bit shy, so let's try to not overwhelm her. Right now, she's working through some identity issues, and our reactions, might motivate her towards a non-socialized response.

CHRIS. Umm, what the hell does that mean?

ANNIE. It means, be chill.

DANIEL. Okay? Let me go get her, she's in the car texting friends.

ANNIE. *(Quietly to Chris.)* Isn't he darling? And I love the way he is so protective of his sister. It's so important to him that she accepts me, and that I get along with her. He's so family oriented. I know it's early to say this, but I really do think I am falling in love.

CHRIS. Oh good. *(Dan enters the front door with Elizabeth. She is provocatively dressed – e.g. boots, fishnet stockings, short shorts, a crop top t-shirt that is cut from the top to show cleavage and from the bottom to show under-bra. Her hair is dyed pink or red or streaks.)*

DANIEL. Chris, Annie, this is Elizabeth. Elizabeth, this is Chris and Annie.

ELIZABETH. *(Shakes hands with Chris.)* Hi Chris. *(Then shakes hands with Annie.)* Hi Annie. *(Then goes back and hugs Chris. Then looks at Annie.)* I like your dress.

ANNIE. Thank you. I like your … shirt.

ELIZABETH. You can borrow it sometime if you'd like.

DANIEL. Elizabeth has restrictions about what she can wear at school. So when she's home she likes to use her own … style … to express herself.

ELIZABETH. Dan likes to make excuses for my bad taste in clothing. Isn't it adorable?

ANNIE. It is really sweet.

ELIZABETH. *(Staring at Annie.)* You're gorgeous. *(She touches Annie's face.)* My god, your face is flawless.

ANNIE. You're making me blush.

ELIZABETH. No, I mean that. Your eyes are mesmerizing. Aren't her eyes mesmerizing, Dan?

DANIEL. It's the first thing I noticed about her.

ELIZABETH. It's a family trait. We love eyes in our family. *(Still staring.)* And your lips, just so supple. Aren't her lips amazing, Chris?

CHRIS. Well, ummm

ELIZABETH. Oh, come on, Chris. You're a fine example of a young, handsome heterosexual male. For sure you've noticed her lips. Right?

CHRIS. They're nice lips.

ELIZABETH. Better than nice. *(Hugs Annie.)* I feel like we are best friends already.

ANNIE. Well, I hope we get to spend some time with each other while you are in town. Maybe we can go somewhere together this week?

DANIEL. You know she's coming to dinner with us tonight right?

ANNIE. Oh … no … I didn't know that.

DANIEL. That's okay, isn't it?

ANNIE. Well, of course. I just think … well, maybe we should change restaurants. Chateau Fontaine has a kind of dress code. I don't think Elizabeth would feel comfortable there in what she has on.

ELIZABETH. I'm comfortable everywhere. This outfit works for all occasions!

DANIEL. We should change restaurants.

CHRIS. Or Elizabeth could borrow one of your dresses. There's a red one that would go great with those boots.

ELIZABETH. I don't have to go with you guys. Honestly. Dan, just drop me off at home. I will be fine.

DANIEL. No. I don't want you to be home alone your first day back.

ANNIE. Dan, you're being overprotective. She's an adult.

ELIZABETH. That's true. I am an adult.

DANIEL. But you suffer from anxiety.

ELIZABETH. That's true too. I do. I suffer from anxiety.

DANIEL. And I'd prefer her not be left alone.

ANNIE. *(A bit let down.)* Oh, okay. That's fine. Why don't I Just change out of this into something more casual.

DANIEL. You don't mind?

ANNIE. Noooo … not at all. I'm just so happy I get to spend time with your sister.

ELIZABETH. Hey guys. How about I just chill out here? Chris would be glad to keep me company. We could watch TV, maybe put on a dirty movie … or watch *(Picks up DVD.)* Love Actually?

ANNIE. That's Chris's favorite movie!

CHRIS. *(To Daniel.)* Not my favorite.

DANIEL. Well, we don't want to impose on Chris.

ELIZABETH. Don't be silly. Chris doesn't have any other plans tonight. Do you, Chris?

CHRIS. Well I …

ELIZABETH. And I need to make new friends. I mean, look at the way I'm dressed, clearly this is a sign that I've been hanging around the wrong crowd.

ANNIE. *(Pleading to Chris.)* Would you mind, Chris?

DANIEL. We don't want to impose.

ELIZABETH. It's no imposition. Chris finds me intriguing, and Annie was looking forward to a big night on the town with her handsome boyfriend. And you're both dressed so lovely, and to be honest I'm tired, and not up for a night out. *(To Chris.)* Chris, I suffer from anxiety, and don't like to be alone in most situations. Would you be my friend and hang out with me tonight? Please?

CHRIS. … sure.

ELIZABETH. Then it's settled! Ken, Barbie, you have a beautiful dinner at Chateau whatever and Chris and I are going to order Pizza and watch some bad rom coms. Annie, can you show me the little girls room? Big decisions like this always make me want to tinkle.

ANNIE. Sure. Follow me. *(They exit down the hallway.)*

DANIEL. You sure you don't mind? She can be a handful.

CHRIS. She's right. I have nothing else to do tonight.

DANIEL. Let me give you some money for the Pizza?

CHRIS. No. I got it.

DANIEL. I gotta be honest. When Annie told me she was breaking up with Bobby today, and I saw you here, I thought you were him. I was afraid it would become a scene. So, I'm kind of glad you'll be here keeping an eye on her house. In case he comes back. Starts any trouble.

CHRIS. I don't think you have to worry about that.

DANIEL. You never know what some people are capable of. I'm sure the breakup destroyed him.

CHRIS. I can guarantee he won't be back.

DANIEL. It's just the way she described him. I was worried he'd be the type of guy that causes a scene, or stalks her, or shows up here with a gun. You know the type. Blustery, immature, needy but heroic in an odd way.

CHRIS. I think her descriptions of people might be off a bit.

DANIEL. Really? Cause usually her descriptions are spot on.

CHRIS. She described me as Gay.

DANIEL. Hmm.

CHRIS. He won't be back. *(Annie and Elizabeth enter from the hallway.)*

ELIZABETH. OK kids, move along. Have a fun night. We'll be here when you get home. *(She kisses Daniel on cheek.)* Goodnight, Danny boy. *(Then kisses Annie on the cheek.)* Goodnight, Annie-Bell. *(Annie starts for door, turns back, and kisses Chris on the cheek.)*

ANNIE. Thank you. *(Annie and Daniel exit out the front door. Elizabeth waits a moment and does a perfect imitation of Annie kissing Chris on the cheek and saying...)*

ELIZABETH. Thank you.

    Blackout.

ACT ONE
Scene 3

Moments later. Outside the house.
Annie and Daniel hold hands as they walk to his car.

ANNIE. Your sister seems … nice.

DANIEL. She dances to the beat of her own drum, that's for sure.

ANNIE. She's so lucky to have you around to look out for her.

DANIEL. It's the other way around really. She looks out for me mostly. It's been just her and me since our mom died, and she's always taken on the role of looking out for me. Even when we were just kids, I'd make a mess and she'd clean it up.

ANNIE. It's hard to picture that. I would have thought it the other way around. She seems kind of a mess, and she's well … you're so crisp and regimented, and she's just … so like a free spirit.

DANIEL. When she needs to be, she's as solid as a rock. She's just going through something right now. Her last relationship didn't end well. He treated her badly and then was out.

ANNIE. Out?

DANIEL. Just up and vanished.

ANNIE. Well you're almost a detective. Couldn't you find him if you wanted to?

DANIEL. *(Deadpan.)* Some people shouldn't be found. He was horrible and trust me when I tell you that's an understatement. I breathed a sigh of relief with him out of her life. Elizabeth took it poorly though.

ANNIE. She misses him?

DANIEL. No. I think she hasn't forgiven herself for falling for him in the first place. She'll work through it. It's just taking a minute. Like I said, I'm usually the one to make the mess, she's usually the one to clean it up. It was even her idea for me to be a cop. She felt like I had a vocation for it.

ANNIE. Well, she's lucky to have you. And I'm lucky to have you too.

DANIEL. Is Chris a good guy?

ANNIE. The best.

DANIEL. You think she'll be okay with him?

ANNIE. He wouldn't hurt a fly.

DANIEL. She's fragile. He wouldn't take advantage of that, would he?

ANNIE. *(Laughs.)* Chris? Lord no.

DANIEL. You sure?

ANNIE. Positive. Chris is an angel.

> *Blackout.*

ACT ONE
Scene 4

Annie's living room.
Elizabeth and Chris are on the couch. An open pizza box is near them.

ELIZABETH. That was the best pizza I've had in ages.

CHRIS. Dominos? You must not get pizza very often.

ELIZABETH. They don't serve it at school.

CHRIS. So what do you study?

ELIZABETH. People.

CHRIS. People?

ELIZABETH. I am an observer of the human condition. Now it's my turn to ask a question.

CHRIS. Okey doke. Shoot.

ELIZABETH. How long have you been in love with Annie?

CHRIS. Pffft. I'm not. I'm not in love with Annie.

ELIZABETH. Yes you are.

CHRIS. You've seen us together for what, four minutes? How do you even come to that conclusion?

ELIZABETH. Because I know what it looks like when you love someone, and they don't love you back. How it feels to be invisible. Or worse, when they know how you feel and get a sense of power from the pain it causes you.

CHRIS. So, you've been there before?

ELIZABETH. A few times. Trust me on this, even with experience it doesn't get easier.

CHRIS. It doesn't matter.

ELIZABETH. But you matter.

CHRIS. But … it … doesn't.

ELIZABETH. But … you … do.

CHRIS. Is that what you learned in school?

ELIZABETH. Don't deflect. You matter.

CHRIS. To whom?

ELIZABETH. … I don't know. But to someone.

CHRIS. But not to Annie.

ELIZABETH. Plenty of Annies in the sea.

CHRIS. Plenty of Dans and Bobbys too. A whole line of guys waiting on Annie, and I seem to be at the back of that line.

ELIZABETH. Ever thought about telling her?

CHRIS. All the time. Do you think I should?

ELIZABETH. Oh, hell no. Forget what you see on TV. Attraction isn't something you can discuss or negotiate. It's a feeling. It takes over. It consumes you.

CHRIS. You won't tell, will you?

ELIZABETH. Your secret is safe with me. Promise. *(A moment.)* Tell me something.

CHRIS. What's that?

ELIZABETH. WHY? Why do you love her?

CHRIS. I … I guess I don't really know.

ELIZABETH. Too easy. Try again.

CHRIS. Because she is a good person maybe?

ELIZABETH. Let's be honest about that. She really isn't. I mean, she's probably okay and all, but she's probably like most people, good when she wants to be, but mainly just … human.

CHRIS. Because she's pretty?

ELIZABETH. Lots of pretty women in the world Chris. I'm pretty, are you in love with me? Nope. So that's not it.

CHRIS. I guess I haven't really thought out the why. Something just clicked when I met her and have no idea why. Whatever she says is interesting, and I try and memorize her every movement so that I can think about it later.

ELIZABETH. So you're infatuated?

CHRIS. I guess so. I just … I love her so much there's almost nothing else I can focus on.

ELIZABETH. You need to re-focus.

CHRIS. Why?

ELIZABETH. Because it's never, ever going to happen. Sorry. Accept it, or you'll make yourself crazy. *(Off his look.)* Trust me on this.

CHRIS. You're probably right.

ELIZABETH. Probably.

CHRIS. But I can still hope, right?

ELIZABETH. Hope is a powerful emotion. And I know that people always say, "Don't give up hope", but most times, it will save you a lot of heartache if you do.

CHRIS. So you're an optimist?

ELIZABETH. A realist.

CHRIS. There someone you pine over?

ELIZABETH. There was. But that's over now. I've learned to accept, to move on.

CHRIS. Just like that?

ELIZABETH. It's a work in progress.

CHRIS. I'm gonna hit the bathroom, then search the kitchen for something to drink. Want a beer or something?

ELIZABETH. No alcohol for me. But if you find another soda … *(Chris exits down the hallway. Elizabeth begins to pace the room, opens a few drawers, looks under the couch, is generally being nosey. She opens the closet and jumps back. She slowly reaches in, and touches Bobby's corpse, maybe feeling for a pulse. She silently freaks out and then jumps back to the couch, staring straight ahead, processing, frozen in fear, or wondering if she is next. After a moment, Chris returns to the room with sodas and sits next to her on the couch).*

CHRIS. Here you go. *(Hands her a soda.)*

ELIZABETH. Thanks. *(Stiff.)*

CHRIS. You okay?

ELIZABETH. Can I ask another question, Chris?

CHRIS. Oh god. Not about Annie. I've just … I'm kind of over that for the day.

ELIZABETH. No, not about Annie.

CHRIS. Okay, shoot.

ELIZABETH. Shoot?

CHRIS. What's your question?

ELIZABETH. What's with the dead guy in the closet?

CHRIS. There's a dead guy in the closet?

ELIZABETH. Chris, you're a horrible liar. Want to try again?

CHRIS. Ohhh yeah … the dead guy. Ummm. That's Bobby.

ELIZABETH. Who's Bobby?

CHRIS. Annie's ex-boyfriend.

ELIZABETH. Ex-boyfriend?

CHRIS. Yeah.

ELIZABETH. How long did they date?

CHRIS. A couple of years.

ELIZABETH. When did it end?

CHRIS. A few hours ago.

ELIZABETH. Did Dan kill him?

CHRIS. No!

ELIZABETH. Did Annie kill him?

CHRIS. No. I think I sorta did.

ELIZABETH. Chris, but … why?

CHRIS. *(Makes it up as he goes along.)* He came in waving his gun at me, pointing it at my head, screaming that if he couldn't have her, no one could. He planned on killing me, then killing her, then killing Dan, then killing himself.

ELIZABETH. So you …?

CHRIS. Kind of saved everyone's life.

ELIZABETH. Oh my god that is so hot.

CHRIS. I mean, I don't want to call myself a hero …

ELIZABETH. Wow … you saved us all.

CHRIS. A man does what a man has to do.

ELIZABETH. *(Jumping up from the couch.)* So let me get this straight … he comes in *(She mimics Bobby.)* and is waving the gun *(Deep voice.)* "I'm gonna kill you, and I'm gonna kill her."

CHRIS. Right, and I stood my ground and said, "No way asshole. You're not going to hurt the woman I love … or her new boyfriend."

ELIZABETH. Oh my god yes …

CHRIS. And then he pointed the gun right in my face.

ELIZABETH. Like this?

CHRIS. Exactly.

ELIZABETH. Then what?

CHRIS. Then he said, "That bitch dumped me, and put all my stuff in the closet." And he opened the door to show me the box.

ELIZABETH. Were you scared?

CHRIS. Fuck no. I thought the gun was a fake and he was bluffing.

ELIZABETH. *(Breathing heavier.)* Was it a fake? Was he bluffing?

CHRIS. No, cause when he came back I got a good look at the gun, and I could see the desperation in his eyes. He told me I would be the first to die. Then Annie. Then DANIEL.

ELIZABETH. Did he mention me?

CHRIS. I don't think he knows about you.

ELIZABETH. Right. Exactly. Of course!

CHRIS. There was a noise outside, so he looked to his left.

ELIZABETH. Like this?

CHRIS. Yes. And then I knocked the gun out of his hand with my left and clocked him on the side of his head with my right.

ELIZABETH. Did he crumble?

CHRIS. He stumbled towards the closet, bent over at the waist, holding the side of his head.

ELIZABETH. Like this? *(She gets into a provocative pose, bent over at the waist, legs spread apart slightly, ass sticking out.)*

CHRIS. Kind of.

ELIZABETH. Is that when you got the gun?

CHRIS. Exactly.

ELIZABETH. And you came right up behind him.

CHRIS. *(He moves closer.)* Yes.

ELIZABETH. Got right up behind him …

CHRIS. *(Gets a bit closer still but still not touching.)* Uh huh.

ELIZABETH. RIGHT ON TOP OF HIM.

CHRIS. *(Positions himself behind her; touching.)* Yeah.

ELIZABETH. And you weren't afraid of him anymore. You were holding the gun.

CHRIS. I had the control.

ELIZABETH. *(Rubs on him.)* His life was in your hands.

CHRIS. It was going to be him or me.

ELIZABETH. He underestimated you.

CHRIS. He did.

ELIZABETH. *(Grinding.)* And you put the gun to his head.

CHRIS. *(Puts a fake gun finger to her head.)* I had him right where I wanted him.

ELIZABETH. Life or death.

CHRIS. Him or me, baby.

ELIZABETH. *(Breathing heavy.)* What did you say?

CHRIS. I said. "Listen motherfucker, I'm gonna make sure you never hurt me or anyone I love."

ELIZABETH. *(Heavy breathing and really grinding now.)* Then what, Chris. Then what did you do?

CHRIS. I felt the cold steel of the trigger on my index finger.

ELIZABETH. There was no going back, was there, Chris?

CHRIS. No going back …

ELIZABETH. And you …?

CHRIS. And I pulled the trigger.

ELIZABETH. Bang *(She falls to the floor, landing on her stomach, rolls over to her back and reaches up so that Chris can lift her up. Instead, she pulls him down on top of her.)*

CHRIS. Well, umm this part didn't happen. *(Elizabeth rolls him over so that he is on his back and she straddles him.)*

ELIZABETH. I am so turned on. We need to make love. Right. Now.

Blackout.

ACT TWO
Scene 1

Annie's Livingroom.

There doesn't appear to be anyone in the room. Suddenly, Chris rises from behind the couch, in boxers and maybe shirtless or wearing a white t-shirt.

CHRIS. That was … *(Elizabeth emerges from behind the couch next to him, wrapped in a sheet.)*

ELIZABETH. *(Singing.)* Amazing!

CHRIS. Amazing.

ELIZABETH. I haven't been that turned on in a long time.

CHRIS. I haven't gotten laid in a long time.

ELIZABETH. Oh that's right, the whole unrequited love thing. Couldn't tell though, you were great.

CHRIS. Thanks.

ELIZABETH. I gotta tell you, that was the best sex I've ever had in my life.

CHRIS. For real?

ELIZABETH. *(Considers.)* Not really. *(She exits down the hallway but leans out to say her next lines. In between her lines, she's searching for something to where from the hallway closet. Maybe clothes are seen flying across the doorway as she searches.)* But it felt good hearing it, didn't it? Best sex I ever had in my life was Freshman year of college. Her name was Lydia and we were in the same dorm.

CHRIS. Oh, you're bi? Didn't realize.

ELIZABETH. Nope. Totally Straight.

CHRIS. But you said … best …

ELIZABETH. *(Now wearing a shirt.)* What can I say, that girl really knew her way around a vagina.

CHRIS. I mean, I don't want to label everything, but doesn't that kind of thing make you bi?

ELIZABETH. *(Now in pants, entering from the hallway.)* No. I don't like vaginas much. I mean, I like mine and all, but on other people, I like dicks. Which, I might add, yours is quite lovely.

CHRIS. I've never heard that before.

ELIZABETH. That's cause you've been banging the wrong type of woman.

CHRIS. What type is that?

ELIZABETH. *(Hugging him.)* The not me type.

CHRIS. I like the you type.

ELIZABETH. And I like the *you* type.

CHRIS. The thing is though, am I going to have to kill someone every time I want to get laid?

ELIZABETH. A girls gotta have her standards.

CHRIS. *(Alarmed.)* You're joking, right?

ELIZABETH. Yes, Chris. I'm not a serial killer. I'm just turned on by powerful men.

CHRIS. I'm not that powerful.

ELIZABETH. More powerful than you realize.

CHRIS. Thank you.

ELIZABETH. No, thank *you.*

CHRIS. So … what do you want to do now?

ELIZABETH. You're joking right?

CHRIS. No.

ELIZABETH. We have to get married.

CHRIS. What?

ELIZABETH. We just had sex. We are in love, and now we should get married!

CHRIS. Umm.

ELIZABETH. Jesus Chris, learn to take a joke. We have work to do. We have to get rid of the body.

CHRIS. Right now?

ELIZABETH. Yes, Chris. Right now. It's gonna start to smell soon. You're lucky the gun was a small caliber. There wasn't even an exit wound. *(They go to closet to look at the body.)* Bullet probably went in, ricocheted off the front of his skull and just rooted around through his brain. Good chance he didn't even die instantly. For sure he had time for one last thought … and you know what his last thought was? *(Whispers in Chris' ear.)* Don't ever fuck with Chris.

CHRIS. That's comforting.

ELIZABETH. His car keys are in his front pocket probably. That's where most guys keep them. *(Chris kneels to retrieve the keys; seems shocked to find them.)* Women's clothing never has pockets. Makes it harder to find the keys after you kill them. They're usually in the purse, but who the hell can ever find anything in a woman's purse, am I right? *(Off his look.)* I'm kidding … but for sure we are going to need to get him wrapped in something so he doesn't leak all over the floor, then we get him to the trunk and get rid of the body.

CHRIS. You've done this before?

ELIZABETH. I watch a lot of TV. *(Not convincing.)* I read a lot of books? *(Still not convincing enough.)* And I may or may not be friends with a few killers. So you have to take my word on it when I tell you that we should probably get him wrapped up in a blanket, get him to the trunk, get rid of the body, and then worry about cleaning out the closet when we get back. I'll drive your car, you can drive his.

CHRIS. Drive it where?

ELIZABETH. Where we are going to dump the body … and the car. Silly.

CHRIS. You really do seem like you've done this before.

ELIZABETH. That's on a need to know basis Romeo and for now, that's nothing you need to know.

CHRIS. I don't think … I think getting you involved in this is a bad idea. This has nothing to do with you.

ELIZABETH. But it does. It's all interrelated. You saved my brother's life, it's the least I can do.

CHRIS. Well I …

ELIZABETH. Shh. Not one more word. Now let's get your sweet little ass moving. Get dressed and lets finish what Annie started.

Blackout.

ACT TWO
Scene 2

Outside the restaurant.

Annie and Daniel are walking back to his car from their fancy dinner.

DANIEL. That dinner was …

ANNIE. *(Singing.)* Amazing!

DANIEL. I haven't had a steak that good in ages.

ANNIE. That steak might have been the best meat I've ever eaten in my life.

DANIEL. *(Innuendo.)* The best?

ANNIE. Well, maybe the second best.

DANIEL. That's better.

ANNIE. Daniel?

DANIEL. Yes?

ANNIE. So, your sister is going to live with you when she's done with school?

DANIEL. Yes.

ANNIE. How would you see that playing out, as in long term? As in … let's say you met a woman and started getting serious with her. And you really liked her. Do you see yourself ever living with a woman?

DANIEL. Sure.

ANNIE. And what if you really fell in love, do you see yourself ever marrying that woman?

DANIEL. Of course. I want the whole thing, the wife, the kids, the house, the dog, the picket fence. How about you?

ANNIE. I want the whole thing too … with the right guy of course.

DANIEL. Of course.

ANNIE. And maybe you might be the right guy. I don't know.

DANIEL. And maybe you might be the right girl.

ANNIE. Sooooo …

DANIEL. What?

ANNIE. How do you see your sister playing into all this?

DANIEL. I'm not sure I get what you mean.

ANNIE. She's not a baby anymore. So when you picture your house with the 2.4 kids and the picket fence, and the 2 car garage, where do you picture your sister?

DANIEL. Elizabeth was all I had after mom died. We took care of each other, we looked out for each other. There's no one in the world I trust more than her, and I am pretty sure she feels the same way. But the thing is, neither of us would ever hold the other one back. She'll always be in my life. But she'd never try to get in the way of my happiness.

ANNIE. That's good.

DANIEL. But also, the right woman for me is going to love her and value her as much as I do. Because she's always going to be in my life. Anything less would be a non-starter.

ANNIE. You're sweet. *(She gives Daniel a tight hug.)*

    Blackout.

ACT TWO
Scene 3

Annie's living room.

At rise, Chris enters from the hallway, hair wet with a fresh shirt on. There is a shovel and maybe a pickax that, after consideration, he puts into the closet. Rubber gloves and bleach sit by the closet door.

CHRIS. *(Talking to himself.)* Well, Chris, you've had quite a day. In the negative column you killed a guy. In the positive column, you made a new friend. In the negative column, the woman you love is now dating someone else. In the positive column, you did get laid. Twice. I kind of feel like we should chalk this one up as a good day. I'll probably get 20 to life for the murder, but who knows, maybe Elizabeth was right and I won't get caught. *(Elizabeth enters from the hallway in a bathrobe and wet tousled hair.)*

ELIZABETH. I have to hand it to you, I thought there was no way you could top our first rendezvous, but you outdid yourself in round two. Definitely gave Lydia a run for her money.

CHRIS. Are you at all concerned that murder seems to turn you on?

ELIZABETH. Maybe I'll bring it up at my next

counselling session. Are you at all concerned that screwing me in Annies's bed seems to really turn you on?

CHRIS. I'll have to bring that up at my next counselling session.

ELIZABETH. You're a good guy, Chris. I know you're busy being helplessly in love with Annie and all, but maybe someday when she's out of your system, we could get together. *(A moment.)* I mean, no pressure, this was what it was. And it was nice, and I 'm not mistaking it for anything real or permanent. Just … this has been fun.

CHRIS. We just disposed of a body. You call that fun?

ELIZABETH. That was work. The rest was fun. I like you.

CHRIS. I like you too. There's something quirky and sweet about you. Wish I could put my finger on it.

ELIZABETH. You put your finger on it a few times.

CHRIS. *(Laughs.)* But yes, I'd like to get to know you better. When do you go back *(Air quotes.)* to school?

ELIZABETH. I'm not sure. I don't want to talk about that.

CHRIS. Okay.

ELIZABETH. I'm going to get dressed. When I get back, let's make out until Dan and Annie get home. Then we can say goodbye.

CHRIS. Okay. *(Elizabeth exits down the hallway.)* What the fuck is wrong with you, Chris? She is the coolest girl you've ever been with. I mean, are you kidding me? She's a dream girl. And here you are still pining for Annie? I mean seriously? Annie is rude, dismissive, and selfish. Elizabeth helped you hide a freaking body. Get your priorities in order, man. *(Elizabeth enters wearing the red dress. She is also wearing the boots she had on earlier.)*

CHRIS. Wow. You look …

ELIZABETH. Do you like the boots? I was gonna grab a pair of heels, but you said earlier that the dress goes with the boots.

CHRIS. I feel like we are going to prom.

ELIZABETH. Prom is over … and you already got laid, sport. And Dan's car just pulled in the driveway.

CHRIS. So our date is over?

ELIZABETH. It would seem so. I get to go back to my life, and you get to go back to being in love with Annie. *(Considers.)* Should I get out of this dress before they come in?

CHRIS. Nah. You look too pretty in it. *(Daniel and Annie enter the front door.)*

ANNIE. Hi, guys. *(Full stop.)* That's my dress.

DANIEL. Wow. Elizabeth, you look fantastic. *(To Annie.)* Doesn't she look great?

ANNIE. You do. You clean up real well. *(Suspicious look to Chris.)* How was your night?

CHRIS. It was …

ELIZABETH. *(Interrupting.)* It was amazing. Chris is such an interesting guy. We've had a great time. I hope you don't mind that I borrowed your dress. Please tell me you don't mind. After a while I just felt so foolish in that silly little outfit I wore, and I wanted to be nice and be pretty, just like you. I don't get a chance to do that very often, be pretty. Please say it's okay.

ANNIE. *(Looking at Daniel, who looks so happy to see his sister cleaned up.)* No. I love it. I wish I had been here to play dress up with you. You look nice. You know what? I'd like it if you'd keep that dress.

ELIZABETH. I couldn't.

ANNIE. I insist.

DANIEL. *(Nearly at a loss for words.)* I cant get over it. *(To Chris.)* I don't know what magic spell you've put on her, but whatever you did, well …

ANNIE. *(Looking at phone.)* Oh, hey Chris, did Bobby ever come by?

CHRIS. Oh yeah, right after you left. Got his box, and split.

ANNIE. Weird. His mom called me. He didn't go home for dinner, and no one has heard from him.

ELIZABETH. No one is gonna either.

ANNIE. What?

CHRIS. Nothing.

ELIZABETH. Chris here is a hero.

CHRIS. You know what, let's just say our goodbyes.

ELIZABETH. What? No. You guys need to know that Chris here is a bona fide hero. *(To Daniel.)* Not at all the little bitch you thought he was gonna be.

CHRIS. What?

DANIEL. I mean I hadn't met you yet. I was just going off Annies's description of you.

ANNIE. I described you as sensitive … but in a good way.

DANIEL. Now you know why I thought you were gay.

CHRIS. I'M NOT GAY.

ELIZABETH. Hell no, you're not! *(High-fives.)*

ANNIE. Wait … did you and he??

ELIZABETH. Hell yeah, we did. Your boy is a hero.

DANIEL. You screwed my sister?

CHRIS. Screwed is such an ugly word.

DANIEL. I left her with you for only a few hours. I said she was fragile.

CHRIS. She's not fragile.

ANNIE. In my bed??

ELIZABETH. And your couch. And your shower. Oh, and where you're standing.

ANNIE. Totally unacceptable, Chris.

ELIZABETH. You all are missing the point. I'm feeling ANXIOUS and NO ONE IS LISTENTING TO ME. Bobby came over with a gun.

DANIEL. Oh my god, are you ok?

ELIZABETH. I'm fine. Chris saved us all.

CHRIS. Well, that might be an exaggeration.

ELIZABETH. Shhhhh. They need to know. Let's tell them everything.

CHRIS. Are you fucking crazy? Your brother is a cop.

DANIEL. Don't call my sister crazy!

ELIZABETH. Don't worry. He'll understand. You didn't do anything wrong.

CHRIS. I think we did. I kind of think we did.

DANIEL. Understand what?

ANNIE. Someone tell me what the fuck happened. Please?

ELIZABETH. *(To Chris.)* You tell it.

CHRIS. Okay, what happened was.

ELIZABETH. What happened was - Bobby came charging in here. His eyes were all red from crying, and bloodshot, and crazy-like. He was waving around a gun the size of a freaking cannon. He screamed at Chris to get up against that wall. Put the gun right up to his head.

ANNIE. Oh my god. You must have been terrified.

ELIZABETH. Are you kidding? Chris? This man has balls of steel! Bobby's plan was to kill Chris, then wait for you to come home, then kill you, and then wait for Dan to come get you for your date and kill him too. But Chris stayed calm and waited for his moment to strike.

ANNIE. Chris did?

ELIZABETH. A sudden noise outside distracted Bobby and, without thinking for his own safety, Chris got the gun with one hand and then punched him with the other. Dropped him like a sack of flour, but Bobby got up again, and put Chris in a chokehold. Chris thought fast and managed to push him back into the wall and break free. After more struggle, and a few more punches, Chris got a hold of the gun and emptied the barrel into Bobby.

ANNIE. You killed bobby?

ELIZABETH. Capped his ass. Taught that thug a lesson he'd never forget. Wait, scratch that. Better line - he ended that motherfucker.

DANIEL. Jesus, Elizabeth, are you ok? Where were you when all this happened?

ELIZABETH. At home with you. It was before we got here.

DANIEL. Before we got here?

ELIZABETH. He was in the closet. Don't feel bad. That's not bad detective work. *(Motherly.)* You're a very good police officer, DANIEL. Don't let this one get to you. He was hidden in the closet.

ANNIE. Wait … so he was dead when I got home??

CHRIS. Yes.

ELIZABETH. *(Exasperated.)* Why does this all seem so hard for you guys to get. Annie broke up with Bobby. Bobby came over to kill everyone. Instead, Chris kills Bobby. Annie comes home. We came over. I mean for god sakes people … it's not that tough a timeline to follow.

ANNIE. So where is Bobby now?

ELIZABETH. We hid the body.

DANIEL. Jesus, Elizabeth. Again?

CHRIS. Wait … what?

DANIEL. Nothing.

CHRIS. No. That's something. What does "again" mean?

ELIZABETH. I've had some … issues in the past.

CHRIS. Issues?

ELIZABETH. Look, I had a life before I met you , okay?

DANIEL. I knew it was a bad idea taking you home for the weekend. There was a reason you were committed.

ELIZABETH. It's a voluntary commitment. I'm allowed to leave whenever I want.

DANIEL. Only because you were never charged with a crime.

CHRIS. Wait … your sister was committed?

ELIZABETH. Voluntary!

CHRIS. To a mental institution?

ELIZABETH. We prefer the term mental health facility.

ANNIE. Ohhhhhhhhh. I get it now. That's why you use air quotes when you say she's "away at school". *(Beat.)* Your sister is fucking crazy!

ELIZABETH. I HAVE SOCIAL ANXIETY AND SOME SOCIOPATHIC TENDENCIES which occasionally lead to RISKY BEHAVIORS, SEXUAL PROMISCUITY, which SOMETIMES results in unintended consequences! I mean really people, who doesn't get that sometimes?

ANNIE. Me. Normal people. People who aren't committed.

ELIZABETH. I'm feeling judged here.

DANIEL. Please don't judge my sister.

ANNIE. *(To Daniel.)* You're a cop. Bobby is dead. Don't you have to do something or something?

DANIEL. I mean, technically … yes, but …

ANNIE. Where the hell is Bobby?

ELIZABETH. We hid the body.

ANNIE. They will find it eventually. And then we'll all be accomplices.

DANIEL. Maybe not. *(To Elizabeth.)* Did *you* hide the body or did Chris?

ELIZABETH. I did.

DANIEL. Will it ever be found?

ELIZABETH. Nope.

DANIEL. You sure?

ELIZABETH. Positive.

DANIEL. Good. *(To Annie.)* The body won't be found.

ANNIE. How can you be sure?

DANIEL. She's good at it.

ANNIE. What???

DANIEL. Some girls can sing. Some girls are good with makeup. Elizabeth is good at hiding bodies. It's a skill.

ANNIE. I don't believe any of this. *(To Chris.)* You killed bobby?

ELIZABETH. I see why brains weren't on your list of why you love her.

ANNIE. And then you and Lizzie Borden hid the body.

ELIZABETH. Calling me Lizzie Borden implies I was involved in the murder. On this one, I just did the cover up.

CHRIS. This one?

ANNIE. *(To DANIEL.)* You, you brought an escapee from a looney bin into my house? So she could fuck my best friend. In my bed.

ELIZABETH. And the shower. And the floor.

ANNIE. Why is she even talking to me? Your sister is insane.

DANIEL. She's not. She just has some issues to work out.

ANNIE. So she worked out her issues by fucking my best friend? Seriously, Dan, how could you not tell me?

DANIEL. You're overreacting.

ANNIE. Am I? Maybe in Casa del Danny killing ex boyfriends and hiding the bodies is business as usual, but in my house it's cause for overreaction.

ELIZABETH. I DIDN'T KILL MY EX BOYFRIEND.

CHRIS. No one said you did.

ELIZABETH. I wanted to, but I couldn't do it. *(To Annie.)* SO DON'T CALL ME A KILLER BECAUSE I'm not.

CHRIS. But you hide the bodies?

ELIZABETH. That's my job. I hide the bodies.

CHRIS. Bodies?

DANIEL. This wasn't her first.

ANNIE. So you've done this a lot? No wonder you're in a nut house.

DANIEL. Stop it. She'd never hurt a fly.

ANNIE. So it's just random happenstance that people keep needing bodies hidden and they come to her?

DANIEL. Things sometimes happen.

ANNIE. Things? You brought a killer into my house.

ELIZABETH. I am not a killer.

ANNIE. Someone killed those people. You helped. That makes you a serial killer.

DANIEL. She's not a serial killer.

ANNIE. Someone sure as hell is.

DANIEL. I AM, OKAY?! *(Long awkward pause.)* Look … back when I was in Middle School there was a guy that lived next door, a few years older than me, and he picked on me mercilessly. One day he followed me out into the woods and started pushing me around. I grabbed a big rock and hit him in the head with it.

CHRIS. You killed him?

DANIEL. Not the first time I hit him.

ELIZABETH. But he was pretty fucking dead by the 7th or 8th time you did.

DANIEL. I'll admit it, I let the anger get the best of me.

CHRIS. I knew it. All cops are fucking crazy.

DANIEL. Yo, sister fucker, you think now is a good time to get smart with me?

ELIZABETH. Danny! Be nice. Anyway … Dan just left the body there, in the open, in the woods. It would have been found in a matter of days, but that's where I came in.

DANIEL. Like I said … she has skills.

ANNIE. If the bully started it, why not just go to the police?

ELIZABETH. Because the self-defense claim kind of goes out the window when the guy's head looks like he fell out of a 30-story building. I had to protect my brother.

CHRIS. So he disappeared?

ELIZABETH. Poof. Gone.

DANIEL. And a few years later, mom died.

ELIZABETH. He didn't kill her. I promise. Sometimes people just die.

DANIEL. Except her dying would have meant we'd be split up since Liz was underage. It made more sense for us to continue as if she was still alive. Just, 'away'.

ELIZABETH. So I handled it. And Dan has taken care of me ever since.

DANIEL. The most recent one was on me, completely.

Just … my bad. Liz was with a guy who put hands on her in the wrong way. So I fixed him.

ELIZABETH. I was unhappy about that one.

DANIEL. Justifiably so.

CHRIS. So Dan is the killer.

ELIZABETH. And I do the cleanup.

DANIEL. There might have been a few others mixed in there. But all for cause.

ELIZABETH. *(Remonstrative.)* How about that guy that took your parking spot?

DANIEL. He saw me waiting there for that spot, and just went around me an took it.

ELIZABETH. You can see now where that one might have been a bit of an overreaction?

DANIEL. I was having a bad day.

ELIZABETH. He always has his reasons … but he's basically a really good guy. You just don't want to be on his bad side.

DANIEL. *(Putting his arm around Chris.)* Chris, you look nervous right now. Rest assured that I didn't kill every guy that has ever slept with my sister. Or even every guy that was disrespectful to her. Just … the last guy did a number on her. It had to be addressed.

ELIZABETH. *(Meek.)* It's what I'm working through now.

DANIEL. I have to protect the people I love. It's just who I am.

ELIZABETH. And I had to protect my brother. He's always been the most stable male role model in my life.

ANNIE. *(Sarcasm.)* Glad we got that straight. Just to be clear … Chris, you're screwing a psychopath, and I'm screwing a serial killer.

DANIEL. Perhaps we should go.

ANNIE. You're all going to prison, you know that right?

ELIZABETH. Only one of us.

ANNIE. What?

ELIZABETH. Only one of us will go to prison. Dan and I have never met Bobby. Nothing tying him to us at all. There's not a drop of Bobby's blood in my house, or in Chris's house. Just … in your house. And I didn't say the police couldn't find the body, only that they wouldn't find the body. But if they DID find the body, they'd find your clothes with your DNA and his blood on them. They might even find some of his blood in your car. Or the murder weapon wrapped in a pair of your unwashed panties. For now, all we have is a missing person, and you have an alibi because you were with DANIEL. So whatever else you do, you'll stay quiet about this whole thing. Nod if you understand me. *(Annie nods.)* We can leave now. I'm tired. It's time for me to go home.

ANNIE. Wait. I want my dress back. *(Elizabeth takes off the red dress, revealing her underwear.)* Is that my underwear? *(Considers.)* You know what? Keep it. *(Daniel and Elizabeth exit out the front door. There's an uncomfortable pause as Annie and Chris stand there.)*

ANNIE. We probably should hang out with each other a lot less.

CHRIS. Agreed.

ANNIE. I guess I should thank you for not letting bobby kill me?

CHRIS. I'm kind of a hero, really.

ANNIE. *(Awkward pause.)* Do you think I was too hard on Dan?

CHRIS. *(Unfuckingbelievable.)* Yes. Yes I do. You should probably go after him. *(Annie exits out the front door.)*

CHRIS. *(Chris pours himself a shot; drinks.)* What was I thinking? What did I ever see in her? *(Elizabeth enters through the front door.)*

ELIZABETH. They're talking. I got cold. *(Chris grabs a throw blanket from the couch and wraps her. It is a sweet gesture.)* Thanks … I heard you talking to yourself. "What did you see in her?" Who is her? Am I her or is Annie her?

CHRIS. Annie is her. For real. What did I see in her?

ELIZABETH. Oh, I was afraid you were talking about me when you said that.

CHRIS. No, I know what I saw in you.

ELIZABETH. What's that?

CHRIS. A really cool girl. Beautiful, smart, funny … and willing to help someone she cares about hide a body. I guess I didn't realize just how much experience you had.

ELIZABETH. Just a few others. And … I've never killed anyone. I mean, if that matters.

CHRIS. It's kind of weird that you got turned on by it though.

ELIZABETH. No one's perfect. *(A moment.)* Dan's going to take me back … to 'school', you know, probably Sunday.

CHRIS. Probably for the best.

ELIZABETH. I guess so.

CHRIS. Was I just … your outlet for promiscuity relating to your condition?

ELIZABETH. No. I really liked you. Remember what you said about attraction? Not understanding it. I felt that with you the second we met. Can't explain it.

CHRIS. No. I get it. I felt it too.

ELIZABETH. You know, if you ever get over being in love with Annie, I could …

CHRIS. I'm over her. I just realized, she's not what I want or what I need.

ELIZABETH. What do you want?

CHRIS. You.

ELIZABETH. I'm only a 30-minute drive away. And I'm voluntary, so we can leave the facility during visiting hours. And I know I've got a lot of work to do, but I am … I am getting better.

CHRIS. Okay.

ELIZABETH. And I'm not crazy you know. *(Chris nods.)* Not too crazy anyway. And I'm not on any medications either. I'm just … a work in progress. *(A car horn honks outside.)* I've gotta go. Will you visit?

CHRIS. Definitely.

ELIZABETH. Promise?

CHRIS. Promise. Maybe even next week … if you want.

ELIZABETH. I want. *(She turns to go but comes back and looks deeply at him.)* If you're really going to visit me, kiss me like you mean it. If you're not, just say goodbye. But don't lie. *(A moment passes. Chris takes her into his arms and kisses her as the lights go dark.)*

END OF PLAY

NOTES

(Use this space to make notes for your production)

NOTES
(Use this space to make notes for your production)

GATHER BY THE GHOST LIGHT
ORIGINAL STORIES FOR RADIO THEATER

GATHER BY THE GHOST LIGHT is a storytelling podcast in radio theater format. Think of the Ghost Light as your campfire. Gather around and listen to stories from a variety of genres. Playwright Jonathan Cook and Devon McSherry are the hosts of the series and most of the stories you hear were originally written as short stage plays and they now have been adapted to audio plays with professional voice actors and immersive sound effects. The audio plays produced on this podcast give these talented playwrights an even wider audience for their stories. We welcome you to join us in this journey as we extend the voices of emerging playwrights!

Available wherever you get your podcasts!
For more information, please visit:
www.gatherbytheghostlight.com
YouTube@gatherbytheghostlight
Instagram@gatherbytheghostlight
Facebook@gatherbytheghostlight